For my mother-in-law Teresa, with love and heartfelt thanks for your boundless generosity and support **—M.F.**
For my grandson, irresistible Uroš **—D.P.**

Published in Canada and the United States of America by Tundra Books, a division of Random House of Canada Limited, a Penguin Random House Company

Library of Congress Control Number: 2014941834

Library and Archives Canada Cataloguing in Publication

Fergus, Maureen, author
InvisiBill / Maureen Fergus ; illustrated by Dušan Petričić.

Issued in print and electronic formats.
ISBN 978-1-77049-613-2 (bound).—ISBN 978-1-77049-615-6 (epub)

I. Petričić, Dušan, illustrator II. Title. III. Title: Invisible.

PS8611.E735I58 2015 jC813'.6 C2014-903054-1
C2014-903055-X

Edited by Tara Walker and Samantha Swenson
Designed by Andrew Roberts
The artwork in this book was rendered in pen and ink and colored in Photoshop.

www.penguinrandomhouse.ca

Printed and bound in China

2 3 4 5 6 20 19 18 17 16

InvisiBill

MAUREEN FERGUS DUŠAN PETRIČIĆ

Tundra Books

If somebody had passed the potatoes
the first time Bill asked for them,
the wonderful, terrible thing
that happened might never have happened.

But nobody did.

"Please pass
the potatoes,"
repeated Bill,
a little louder
this time.

*Nobody even
looked at him.*

Bill's mother (a busy woman with an
important job) was busy discussing
something important with his father
(an important man with a busy job).

Bill's big brother was
reading a favorite
textbook,

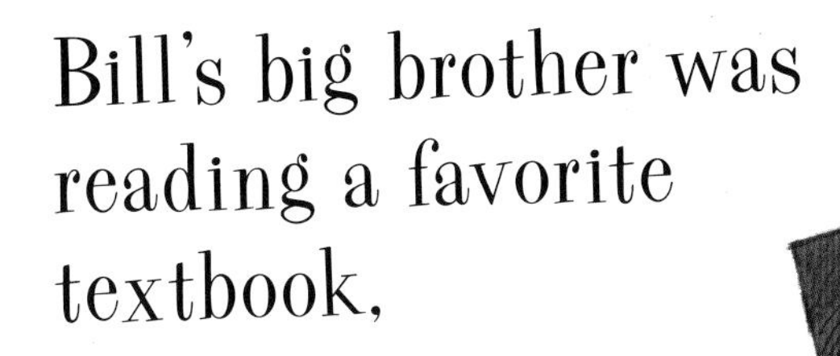

and his little sister was watching
world class juggling on TV.

"What am I,
invisible?"
muttered Bill.

"PASS THE POTATOES!"

"Eat your potatoes, dear," said his mother as she checked for messages on her whatchamacallit.

"Watch your tone, mister," said his father as he answered his thingamajiggy.

“The scientific name for potatoes is SOLANUM TUBEROSUM,” said his brother. “They’re considered edible tubers.”

“Oh,” said Bill. “Well, pass the edible tubers.”

Bill's sister reached for the edible tubers, but instead of passing them to Bill, she started juggling them.

She was so good that Bill's mother, father and brother all stopped what they were doing to watch her.

It was then that the terrible thing happened...
Bill turned invisible.

Even worse, nobody noticed until it was time to clear the dishes.

"Where's Bill?" asked his brother and sister, who did not want to get stuck clearing the table by themselves.

"I'm right here," said Bill, waving his arms.

But, of course, no one could see him or his arms.

"What is the meaning of this behavior, young man?" demanded his father.

"Turning invisible is not behavior," said Bill.

"What are we going to do?" cried his mother.

"Call the doctor," said his father. "And stay calm. Bill is probably just looking for attention."

The next morning, Bill's mother took him to see Dr. Buttlington.

After describing Bill's symptoms, which included invisibleness and a bit of an attitude, his mother said, "This is just like the time his cousin Clarissa got the chicken pox."

"Turning invisible is nothing like getting the chicken pox," said Bill.

Doctor Buttlington agreed.

"Turning invisible means that a person can't be seen," he explained solemnly. "Chicken pox are little red dots on the skin."

"I see," said Bill's mother. "Is there anything we can do?"

"A strong dose of permanent markers should do the trick," said Dr. Buttlington.

After praising Dr. Buttlington's wisdom,

Bill's mother took Bill home
and used an orange marker
to color his face and a green
marker to color his hair.

Then
she ran
out of markers.

“I can’t go to school
looking like this!” said Bill.

“Don’t be so concerned
about how you look,”
said his mother.

“Be proud of who you
are on the inside.”

But at that particular moment, Bill didn't care about who he was on the inside. What he cared about was what the other kids were going to do when they saw his floating pumpkin head.

And what they did was laugh.

Whether he was playing tag at recess or performing his trumpet solo in music class or diving off the high board during swimming lessons,

they laughed...

and laughed...

and laughed...

By the end of that long, hard day of being laughed at,
Bill was in no mood to eat dinner with his family
who had, after all, caused his invisibleness.

So he took three peanut-butter-and-pickle sandwiches up to his room and spent the evening with his gerbil, Gerard. Together, they cooked up a plan to make Bill's family sorry for what they'd done.

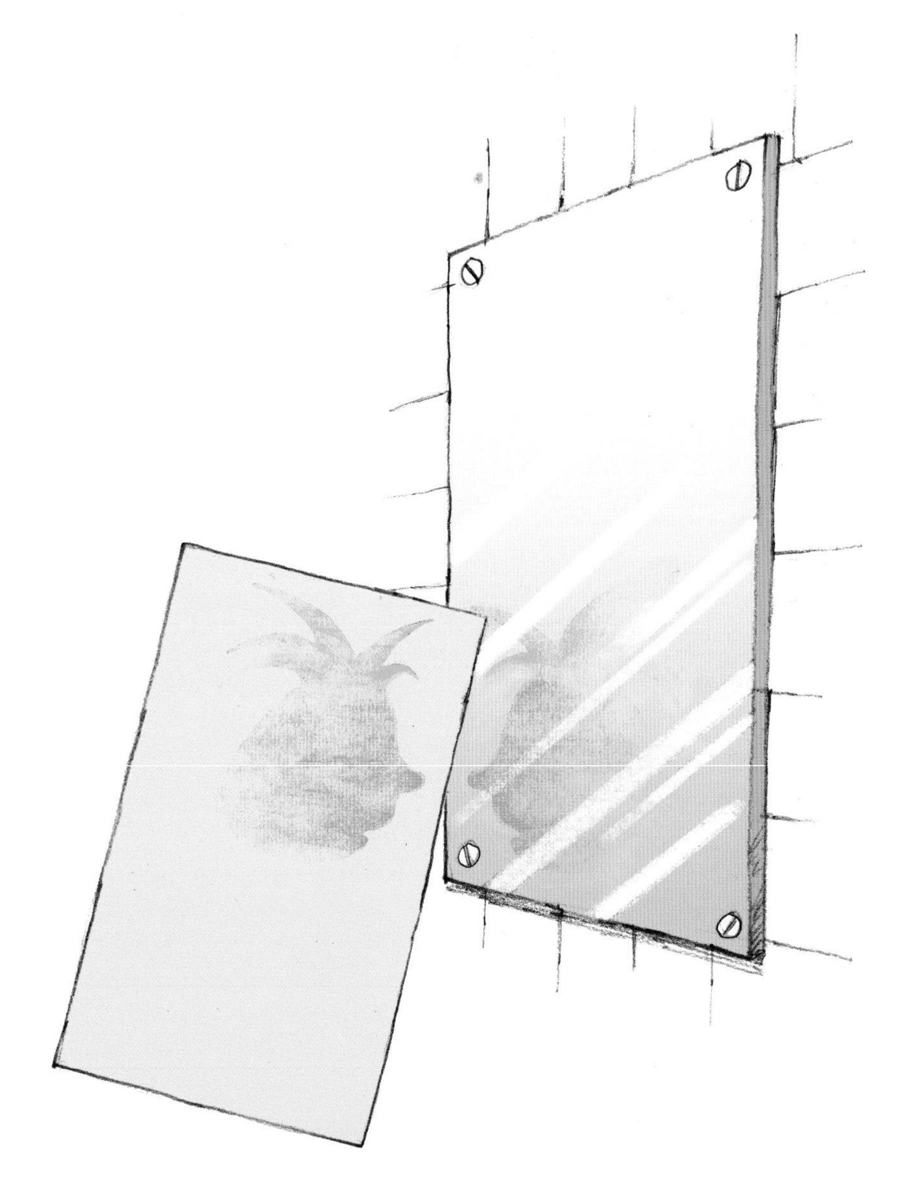

The next morning, Bill put
his plan into action.
While his mother
and father and brother
and sister were
rushing around
getting ready for
their busy, important
days, Bill tiptoed
into the bathroom
and scrubbed his
head clean.

Then he wrote
a note to
his family:

Bill put the note
where he knew his
family would find it.

Then he waited for somebody to notice
that the floating pumpkin head
was not rushing around getting
ready for *his* busy, important day.

He waited...
and waited...
and waited...

Finally, just as everybody was about to hurry out the front door, Bill's mother remembered that it was garbage day.

"Where's Bill?" asked Bill's brother and sister, who did not want to get stuck taking out the trash by themselves.

This time, Bill didn't say, "I'm right here," *or* wave his arms.

Instead, he held his breath and watched to see what would happen.

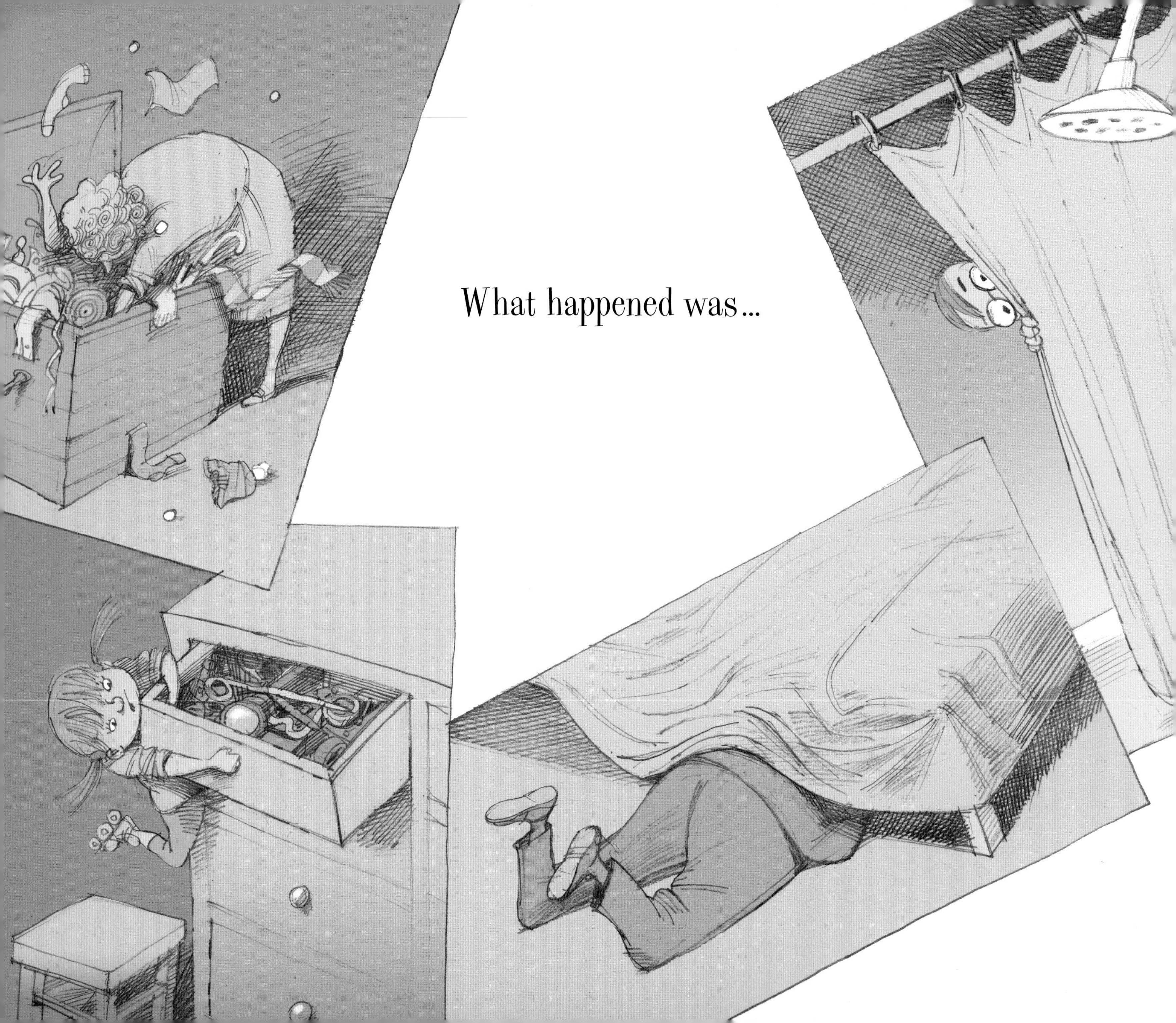

What happened was...

...his family spent

A LOT

of valuable time
looking for him.

When they found Bill's note,
they got so worried that...

Bill's mother didn't
notice her
whatchamacallit
buzzing...

and his father didn't hear his thingamajiggy beeping...

and his brother's eyelids started to twitch...

and his sister's teeth began to chatter.

As he watched his family fret,
Bill hugged himself hard and
smiled a big, invisible smile because
even though he knew it wasn't nice
to worry his family in this way,
he couldn't remember the last
time they'd talked and thought
about nothing but *him*.

Then Bill's mother started crying and said it was her fault for making him go to school looking like a floating pumpkin head.

His father started crying and said it was his fault for saying that turning invisible was attention-seeking behavior.

His brother started crying and said it was his fault for telling Bill the scientific name for potatoes.

His sister started crying and said it was her fault for juggling the edible tubers that Bill had wanted to eat.

Right about then, Bill started crying because it was *his* fault that his mother and father and brother and sister were crying.

And even though they were often too rushed or too distracted to pay proper attention to him, they were paying proper attention to him *now.*

It was then that the wonderful thing happened:
Bill turned visible again.

Even better, everybody noticed right away.

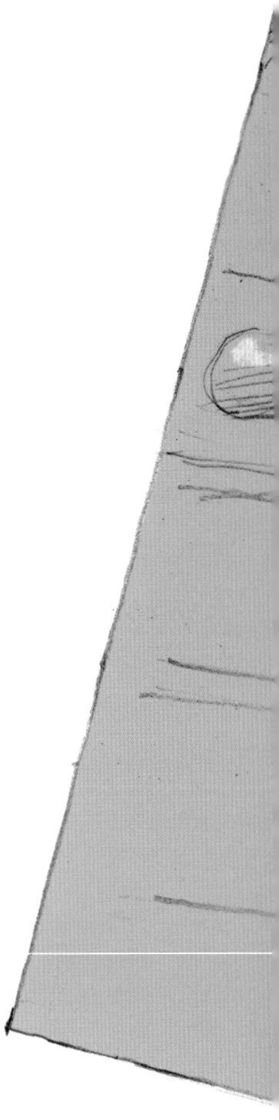

"I'm so happy you're back!" cried Bill's father.

"Dr. Buttlington is a genius!" cried his mother.

"It's your turn to take out the garbage," said his brother and sister.

"I know it is," said Bill.

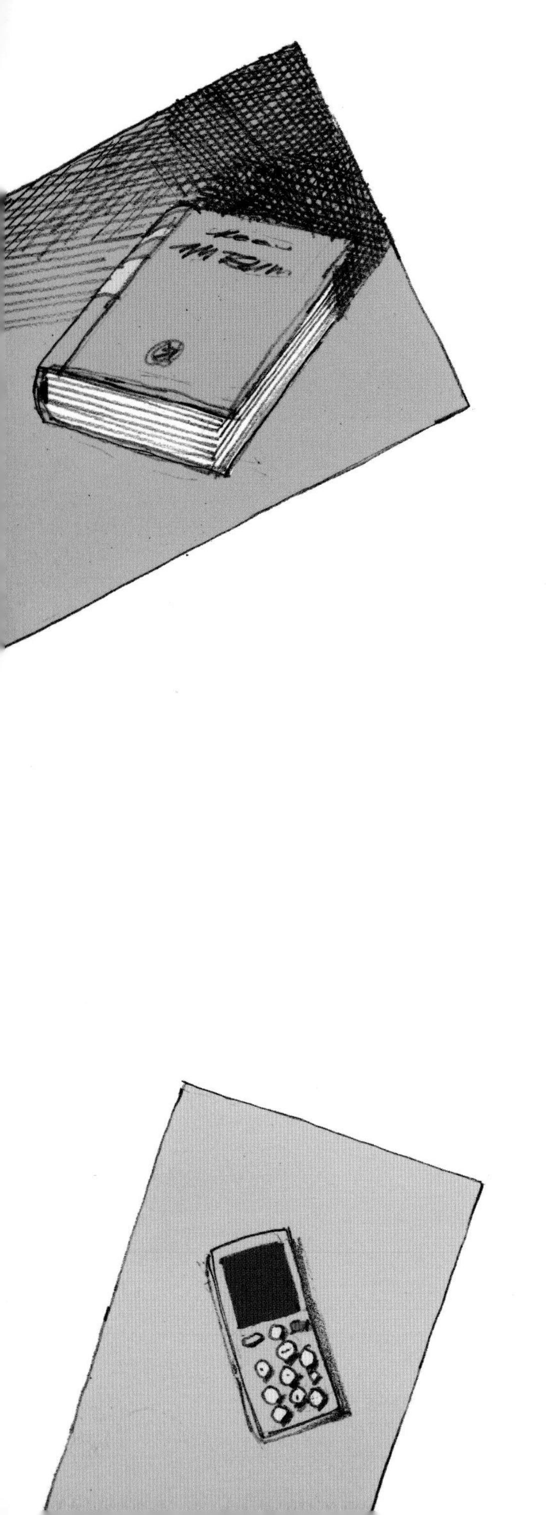

That night before they sat down to dinner,
Bill's brother closed his favorite textbook,
and his sister turned off the TV.
His father powered down his thingamajiggy,
and his mother put away
her whatchamacallit.

For a moment, all was quiet and calm.

Then Bill's mother smiled at him and said, "Would you like me to pass the potatoes, dear?"

"Yes," said Bill. "That is *exactly* what I would like."